D0294971

02955

Leah Komaiko

Leonora O'Grady

ILLUSTRATED BY LAURA CORNELL

VIKING

VIKING

Published by the Penguin Group
Penguin Books Ltd, 27 Wrights Lane, London W8 5TZ, England
Penguin Books USA Inc., 375 Hudson Street, New York, New York 10014, USA
Penguin Books Australia Ltd, Ringwood, Victoria, Australia
Penguin Books Canada Ltd, 10 Alcorn Avenue, Toronto, Ontario, Canada M4V 3B2
Penguin Books (NZ) Ltd, 182–190 Wairau Road, Auckland 10, New Zealand

Penguin Books Ltd, Registered Offices: Harmondsworth, Middlesex, England

First published in the USA by HarperCollins 1992
First published in Great Britain by Viking 1992
1 3 5 7 9 10 8 6 4 2

Text copyright © Leah Komaiko, 1992
Illustrations copyright © Laura Cornell, 1992

The moral right of the author and illustrator has been asserted

All rights reserved. Without limiting the rights under copyright reserved above,
no part of this publication may be reproduced, stored in or introduced into a
retrieval system, or transmitted, in any form or by any means (electronic,
mechanical, photocopying, recording or otherwise), without the prior written
permission of both the copyright owner and the above publisher of this book.

Filmset in 19pt Goudy Bold

Printed by Imago Publishing Ltd, Hong Kong

A CIP catalogue record for this book is available from the British Library

ISBN 0–670–84225–7

*In memory of Dorothy Komaiko,
my mother and Leonora's biggest fan – L.K.*

For Gram – L.C.

LEONORA O'GRADY
Has a bouquet of rags
That she gardens each morning
In six shopping bags.

And they bloom in a cart
That she pushes around
And it's stacked to the sky
With the things she has found ...

Old spaghetti jump ropes
A bottle of ants
A necklace of acorns
The queen's underpants

Popcorn from Paraguay
Snakeskins from Spain
A buffalo's toothbrush
A full tube of rain!

A whistling alarm clock
A snoring teakettle
An ostrich's knee socks
One bulldozer pedal

Mud mugs, two glass rugs
A marmalade hat
And on top of the pile sits
Leonora's pink cat!

Treasures you won't find inside the museum
So why doesn't everyone want to come see them?

She doesn't have money
To buy much to eat
So she saves up each week
For her favourite treat.

She goes to the baker
For a slice of corn bread
And she takes a taste –
Puts the rest on her head.

Then in flock the crows
Single file and polite

And each has his turn
To take one birdie bite,
And this makes Leonora's eyes happy and bright.

Leonora's house is next to Riverview Park
And she lives all alone
Until just after dark.

Then she pulls out her shawl
And her best cobweb stocking

And in no time she's got
That whole sleepy park rocking!

For that's when she brings
Her whole family to life,

She's the moon shadow's daughter
The old statue's wife.
And together they tango
Around the old square
While the spiders weave lilies
For Leonora's sweet hair.

And some nights she falls asleep
Under the willow.
The dew is her blanket,
The clouds are her pillow.

And then the next morning
The squirrels think they may
Wake up Leonora and then run away.

She's somebody special
And here's how I know,
When I say "Good morning"
She calls back
"Hello."